foxing the witch

pentagrammatically speaking

john sellers

ꝼor
anꝺrew
anꝺ
john

specíal
thanks
to
heíꝺí
anꝺ
colín

ISBN 1- 885003-22-6
Library of Congress Catalog Card Number: 98-86703

Foxing The Witch / written and illustrated by John Sellers

First Edition
Copyright 1999 by John Sellers
Printed in Hong Kong

foxing the
witch

john sellers

llhallows Eve. Fox was caught by a sudden storm that sprung like a steel trap. He sheltered uneasily below the ancient stone bridge shading the cold, swift brook sweeping past a briar-hedged lawn. A place of evil reputation. Witching Bridge it was called, for here it was said that the witch, eleven-fingered Mab, who dwelt in the house on the hill, would come to fish for bewildered souls of the dead as they were swept downstream and out to sea. For the moment, lightning crack and thunder's rumble were his only companions as Fox looked nervously toward the house which loomed like an old tombstone. He sought distraction by flipping cards into a hat. Then green lightning cast a monstrous shadow down upon the wet bankside. The wild, black hair of the witch, streaming with rain, shrouding the crown of the bridge, seemed to reach for him. A card he had just cast floated up to her on a spiraling gust. She caught it. The fool card with the face of a fox leered at her. Her hand twitched. The card dropped, flittering spiral of a maple spinner, falling into the bottom of the hat. Fox looked up and spoke these words:

There once was a fox in the wood,
looking for more than he should,
he met a young witch
with a curious twitch,
while he took as much as he could.

"Ordinarily, I don't twitch," said Mab. "I am sure you don't."

Fox retrieved the cards from the hat, and began shuffling the deck with clever paws.

"Risk, chance, destiny. Tricks, hazards, bluffs. Conceal the past and foretell the future while idling away the present. Do you look for love? Let cards reveal your desire. Or does the glitter of wealth color your dreams tonight?"

"It is harvest time," Mab answered. "Tonight I fill a bag of souls to hang up in my root cellar for the winter. But a fox gilded with red and silver should know that. And also know better than to play games under this bridge on this night. There is room for you in my sack. Come, you are the first catch of the night."

"If I were to tell you how you came by that eleventh finger, would you spare me?" begged Fox, playing for time. "Picture this— mother sends child to the garden before dinner. Child reaches into a bush to pick a green cucumber. A diamond-banded snake scales her arm, coiling around her wrist. Child cries out. Now see the hand yanked from the bush. Child looks at snake. Snake looks at child. Snake becomes finger, as if born to her sacred left hand, the common telltale for every witch since the beginning of the world."

Mab's wide eyes unmasked her curiosity.

"How do you know that?"

"Perhaps the snake was not the only one lurking in the garden that day. No? Then it must be the telling of the cards," Fox said as he dramatically plucked a card from the deck.

4

"Regard. The dark Wizard. Most unfortunate for you. And what is this?"

Fox drew another card.

"Raven. Blacker than blackest night. Minion to the Wizard and set by that evil conjuror to spy upon you in your most private moments," Fox's voice shrunk to a whisper as he glanced about, conspiracy simmering in his eyes; sly, red tongue curled with caution.

ab was so charmed by Fox's memory of her childhood secret that a duet of salt tears painted her eyes. Yet it was Fox whose vision was strangely blurred. Somehow the witch had come down from the bridge and stood before him. Startled, he dumped the cards into the hat, clapped the hat on his head and backed into the shadows under the bridge. But now she was behind him. Her six-fingered left hand pinched his soggy red tail, provoking a squeak through his teeth.

"Your story touches me," Mab smiled. "I would requite you in my own way."

She leaned close, showing Fox the sprig of fennel held in her other hand.

"But the Wizard..."

"Remove your hat that I may place a blessing upon your wise head with this pleasant fennel."

Fox frowned, knowing that if the witch struck him with fennel, he would fall to her enchantment, and soon be bundled in her hunting sack along with other hapless souls of this troubling night.

"Perhaps later," he replied. "First, how about a quick game of *Heart On Your Sleeve*?"

"I don't play cards," Mab demurred.

"Ah, but you already have. Look at your sleeve. Queen of Hearts. Am I right?"

Mab discovered a paper card tucked in her sleeve. Rain drops dripped down the twin faces that mirrored her own. She released Fox to extract the card.

"Clever. Perhaps I am mistaken, but isn't this the Queen of Clubs?"

"The trick needs some work," Fox's brow furrowed with annoyance. "Mind you, there are places in this wicked world where being caught with a card up your sleeve can lead to serious difficulty."

"Yes, it is a wicked world," Mab thoughtfully agreed. "Better to depart it."

She opened her black sack. Fox doffed his derby and caught the falling deck of cards. Six cards escaped his grasp to form a crescent upon the damp ground.

"Behold! Wizard and Raven return to haunt your path. As for these others..."

A splash of lightning caught Fox furtively glancing up to see if he had finally captured Mab's attention. And, indeed, he had done so.

"What of the others?" she demanded.

"Seven cards in all. Two we know. One missing— held by you. And these..." Fox said as he deliberately culled the remaining four.

The Dragon old, the Fairy cold,
Count each ancient emblem.
The Turtle jailed, the Lady veiled,
A witch's hand to bind them.

Fox dropped the cards back in the hat. He turned the hat over, but nothing fell out.

"Ha! Where are they?" Mab was intrigued. "I must know the secret. What does it mean?"

"Very well. A hint," Fox carefully positioned the hat back on the ground and beckoned.

"Drop the Queen here."

Mab took a small step forward.

"Quickly," Fox urged.

Mab bent to peer into the hat. Her red nails fanned out like a tropical bloom.

The Queen of Clubs spun toward the hat, but Mab had not let go. No, it was she who was falling; falling into the hat.

"What...." was all she could gasp.

"Oops!" Fox laughed. "My mistake."

m ab tumbled into the hat. She fell screaming through a black tunnel to emerge in a great, glowing volcanic chamber wormed into the heart of a nameless mountain. Here the journey abruptly ended with a clumsy dive into a heap of richly embroidered carpets, raising plumes of dust.

A ruddy glow bled weakly throughout the cavern, revealing an unexpected stash of treasure, doubtless the fruits of centuries of pillage. Here a cache of jewels, there stolen gold. Iconic wisdom remembered in stacks of holy, stained glass windows. Sprawled in the center of the dusty glitter lay a dragon, lost in a profound, reptilian trance. Mab grabbed her nose in time to stifle a huge, whooping sneeze.

"The Dragon old?" Mab wondered. Why had Fox worked this trick, placing her in mortal danger? Her green eyes searched the dark for an escape, but discovered the Queen of Clubs still clutched in her hand. Disdainfully, she discarded it. The card touched the floor, scarcely raising the ghost of a sound, but it was enough. The creature blinked a long, slow blink. Mab froze, posing herself as a painted statue.

Dragon shook his head and yawned painfully. He stared intently at the card on the floor. His penetrating gaze, slit eyes sheltering dying embers, pierced the shadows, disconcerting Mab, who felt pinned and etherized like a butterfly. With a convulsive snatch of the card, Dragon slithered arthritically to a shelf where

lay a large briar pipe. He dragged a flinty talon across the rock wall, catching a shower of sparks in the bowl and puffing the pipe into pungent life. One deep draw. A second. He crumpled the card and shoved the wad into his pipe where it briefly flared. Flinging the pipe aside, Dragon gasped and flopped upon the stone floor, wet spasms of coughing echoing in the vast chamber, slowly subsiding, relieved by a noisy wheeze. Chill, stale air howled into his nostrils and blew out again, each breath seeming his last. Mab clung to her sheltering carpets. Finally, Dragon, intimate with every detail of the room, down to the least mote of tainted wealth, addressed the intruder, his voice a groaning, rusted hinge.

"I have not dined in... memory fails. Once I would have found you a most exotic delicacy... poisonous witch flesh... quite an addiction for your kind... savory violet blood... but no need for alarm. I've quite lost my appetite. Admire, if you will, these yellowed teeth depending uncertainly from feeble gums. Humorless cancer clenches my gut. Lung-rotted, senile beast holed up in a cold crater. Pitiable.

"I am seldom, almost never, favored with visitors," he continued. "Access to this den is difficult, or impossible, but for a witch such as you, one who can fly a broom under the pitiless glow of cold moon and indifferent stars."

Mab had never seen a dragon before. Rumor held that her mother (another Mab, another story) had been taken by a dragon. Likely

this one? Had Fox conjured her here with the intent that Dragon make a breakfast of her? Why? Though Dragon might be dying as claimed, he was no less dangerous. She must choose artful words, crafting a way to make her escape. But how to enchant a creature hatched long before witch ever cast spell in this world? Mab summoned a sweet smile.

"Witches do not fly on brooms."

ragon pondered. "Of course. I might have suspected as much. I should have seen a witch fly at some time. Unnatural. Who would clutch a crooked stick of hickory between a pair of bony knees, attempting flight? Now answer this— how did a beauteous, young witch enter my lair?"

Mab told of her encounter with Fox. Dragon gagged on a tidal torrent of laughter.

"Foxed! The witch foxed!" Dragon roared with youthful vigor reborn. Mab's smile thinned as she pretended to shrug away the humiliation.

"Yes, that grieves you. Fox is a lying, thieving trickster. Count those among his virtues. Can I share a matter of confidence?" A wavering talon over his sharp mouth commanded secrecy.

"He foxed me as well," Dragon coughed out a dead chuckle. It bubbled from his cracked lips like soured milk on full boil. He shifted his ponderous bulk; greedy claws rummaging through metallic waves of riches.

"I, too, have played the thief. But my acquisitions have been gleaned with the strictest of curatorial eyes. As for the fire-breathing, the destruction, the plundering— "

"The slaying of witches," Mab injected.

Dragon paused to weigh truth and sarcasm.

"Existence tends to be a messy business," he decided. "Especially you who are so comely, so delicious, so cruel, need not be told. Had but we met a century ago... well, had I tears I would weep. Now, what point was I making?"

"That you are misunderstood," Mab ventured. She was feeling quite comfortable, lounging on her mound of moldy rugs. "Shall I prescribe for you a distillation of herbs to restore memory, repaint vision, revive appetite? Henbane for asthma, blue lobelia for nerves."

"You would poison me?"

Mab nodded cheerfully.

"Excellent. We do understand each other. But concerning our mutual friend. Reluctantly, I confess he has stolen sundry items. An odd piece of haberdashery. Specifically a hat. Deck of cards. Merest of trifles. Yet, I am pained to have the least part of my treasury disturbed."

"The hat I fell into?"

"Beauty embraced by wisdom," Dragon marveled. "I think I shall not part with you, my jewel of jewels, my lady of crimson dreams."

"Your business is with Fox," Mab frowned. "Pure accident brings me here."

"Indeed. And history is but the telling of accidents. Fox is not here. You are. Oh, very well. A fair proposal— I set you free. Find and deliver Fox to me. Or stay. As my permanent guest. Yes, perhaps better that you remain..."

Not one to let opportunity grow lonely, Mab gave quick consent, resolving that once away she would do as she pleased. Let Dragon die. She would deal with Fox in her own right.

"Ah, you contemplate evasion," Dragon winked. "Betrayal. An ugly word. But curiosity will chastise faithlessness. The rush of event

will keep you true to the path. Your quest awaits. Come. Enthrone yourself."

Dragon lowered his head. Puzzled and wary, but wishing escape, Mab mounted Dragon's scaly armor, nesting painfully on a thorn-tiled skull, scraping her skin to find a grip. He snaked his way up a dark shaft, pitching and rolling his passenger, finally, emerging in a dead crater canopied by a starry night.

There was a groaning and creaking of framework wings; leathery hooks fastening upon the air. An icy rush of air unfurled Mab's hair. Unexpectedly, Dragon shot up past the limits of the night sky toward the forbidden heavens. Alarmed, Mab tried to shout, but a hateful, frigid wind stole her voice. She beat upon Dragon's head, managing only to hurt her hands. Then out into the stellar void with Dragon's snout aimed at the moon.

Mab remembered that a dragon must never fly at night because the moon would charm him as candle flame does the moth. And so it was that witches favored the night to avoid the dragon's predatory eye. Soon the lunar sphere swung down at them like a silver pendulum. Dragon sailed near and a violent shake of spasm-stricken wings sent Mab spilling from his head to a rock-hard landing. Just before losing consciousness, Mab witnessed tail-biting Dragon looping drunkenly, back down to the world.

When she awoke the moon had gone from full to a fine sliver in the night sky. Her face broke into an unsatisfying yawn as she stretched to find the ache that plowed her spine. She was balanced precariously between the horns of the moon; cold, bare legs straddling the crescent. A spider of crystal dangled from a silken strand of moonbeam above her head.

"Go away!" Icy needles in her ears.

"What?" Mab's voice was painfully loud, resonating like a drum beat. The moon shuddered as if it were a glassy ship running aground in a sea of glacial coral. The legs of the Crystal Spider shook and rattled like wind-strewn icicles.

"Whoa!" cried Mab, who had never ridden a horse in her life. The lurching motion subsided. Mab held on tightly, fearful of falling off into space. Her hands clutched a brittle weave of curved crystal strands whose pale glow painted her skin and seeped into her bones.

"Silence! You disrupt everything!"

"The moon is a spider web? Or do I dream? Who are you? How can this be?"

Now the spider paused in its spinning, profoundly irritated for it had never been so questioned since the birth of time.

"I weave the eighths, the quarters, the halves and wholes that mark time. The celestial measure is my doing and undoing. Now leave."

"Gladly," Mab conceded. "But how?"

"Go to the sun with your questions. Begone!" The spider closed its jeweled eyes and ceased all motion. The moon's glow diminished, leaving Mab hanging on the edge of oblivion. Then Fox's voice whispered out of the dark:

There once was a fox in the sky,
stealing stars from heaven's blue eye,
the witch caught him there,
ascending the stair,
where he took all that he could spy.

This was exceedingly strange. Mab could see Fox suspended nearby in the lunar chill, eyes and teeth agleam, grinning merrily at her.

"You are probably wondering how I happen to be here. Well, it seems that while loitering by an oak tree, I saw Dragon convey you skyward and moonbound. Noticing that the topmost branches of the tree seemed to touch the moon, it seemed to me that I might be able to climb up and see how you were doing. So tell me dear Mab— how are you doing? Having a bit of trouble?"

ab gingerly slid down the sharp-shanked moon toward Fox, smiling as if he were the dearest of friends. She leaned and stretched out her arm, beckoning to him, longing to fasten her red nails in his furry pelt and yank him onto the moon with her. Yet, though he seemed to be so near, she could not touch him nor could her fingers even find trace of branch or leaf.

"Careful, Mab. Don't fall off."

"Why can't I reach the tree? Or you?"

"As I was trying to explain: the perspective from the base of the tree places the branches next to the moon," Fox mused. "But for someone actually on the moon— such as yourself— the familiar astral relationships revert to form."

"Meaning?"

"Big creek. No paddle," Fox shrugged.

"This is your doing! You conspired with Dragon to trap me here."

"Not at all. I came to rescue you. None too soon it seems. Bit unstable. Not exactly what I expected. As for Dragon bringing you here— well, what do you expect? Flying a dragon under moonlight," Fox shook his head. "A witch should know better. Besides, you tried to steal my soul. Bit of drollery on your part, I suppose? And now you blame me for your troubles."

"Yes. A harmless jest for Allhallow's Eve. I doubt you have a soul worth the taking."

"You wound me," Fox pouted. "To think I have climbed all the way to the moon to be insulted. Ingrate. I should abandon you now, but it just won't do to let you bring the universe to a grinding halt." Fox turned to scan the infinite darkness from his oaken loft; red tail waving in Mab's face. "It is rather pleasant to sit back and enjoy the big picture."

"Pay attention!" Mab cried, causing the moon to moan and shake. "How do I get down from here?" her voice shriveled to an hysterical whisper. "What of the spider and time? The moon is coming apart!"

Fox turned back to speak, but a sudden tremor shook the oak tree, flipping him over then back again. Somehow he held on. Now, it was Fox's turn to be agitated.

"The situation appears to have developed a certain gravity. Would it be too much to expect that you have an old broom handy?" Fox squeaked, urgency throttling him like a vise.

Mab did not bother to reply, a cloud of black thoughts infesting her mind. Witch and Fox sat in silence, contemplating the imminent conclusion of the universe. Sympathetic to the witch's poisonous mood, seven stars fell from their assigned places, dissolving like guttering fireworks. Others shimmered violently, threatening to shatter. All of space looked flat and brittle, curled and flaking, as if it were a crumbling, faded sheet of wallpaper. Mab's black thoughts boiled and swirled, giving birth to a swarm of twittering black bats, so black as to blot even the uttermost darkness of space.

The swarm closed upon her like a fisherman's net and lifted her into the eternal lunar night.

"Awaken Crystal Spider," Mab begged. "Spin your moonbeams again."

The stain of witchcraft removed, the Crystal Spider shook off fatal lethargy, hurrying to make up for lost time, spinning a fresh new moon, while a much relieved Fox descended the tree.

s the swarm swept Mab from the moon, she could not enjoy the splendor of the world's green orb dangling nearby, a brilliant ornament amid the dazzle of white stars. The bats, though under compulsion of her enchantment, were discontent in this dull labor. Their attention wavered, they argued and fought, scratching Mab's skin, tearing her gown and tangling her hair. It was a bumpy, queasy ride, and she wished for an end to it. The bats improvised a dire lullaby, giving them strength to descend with this unaccustomed burden, driving Mab into fretful slumber.

> *Tug her, lug her, frisk her, risk her,*
> *clap her, flap her, nip her, trip her,*
> *stick her, prick her, slide her, glide her,*
> *flip her, clip her, knock her, pock her,*
> *make her, take her, feel her, peel her,*
> *crop her, drop her, tap her, snap her,*
> *pick her, nick her, bite her, kite her,*
> *lift her, gift her, jump her, dump her.*

But the dawning sun burst over the rim of the world, and Mab's spell was consumed in rude sunlight. The bats were scattered into dark dust. Mab fell. Her gown, much tattered from her ordeals in Dragon's lair, on the moon and by the careless handling of the bats, was ripped from her back like plucked wings. The world bounded topsy-turvy past her eyes. She fell through a realm of purple clouds and into the promise of a brief and final morning. Hard ground beckoned. Mab's lips spouted prayer.

"If— if I survive— if I survive, I vow— "

But prayer was cut short; vow aborted. Mab was yanked to a halt, a single finger hooked by a darting, blue-skinned fairy whose shining silver feathers beat madly. Mab was dazzled by the painful brightness. A voice sounding a pleasant peal of musical bells stroked her ears.

"You wander far from home, daughter of the snake. Wounded and filthy as you are— gross of body, your soul bruised and heart soiled— I embrace you. Come dwell in my cloud palace, where a hundred sprites and winged imps wait to attend your desire. Your vulgar form will attenuate until pure and light. This tangled, shadowy cloak of hair will metamorphose to black, velvety wings, never to brush the earth again but when we sip sweet nectars from morning blossoms. And then..."

As Fairy sang, a pleasing vista was revealed to Mab, a place of golden clouds clasped by sky of heraldic blue, adorned with songbirds of every feather and sprays of dusky butterflies. Though all she saw and felt was utterly alien, an odd notion of redemption transpired, and Mab might well have chosen this new and unexpected path. However, the mention of nectar gave birth to a vicious complaint from her stomach, reminding the witch that a meal was long overdue. Suddenly, Mab hated this bright, impertinent creature. She was curious to know what the flavor of blue might be. Cat-quick, Mab stuffed screeching Fairy into her

mouth; small, silver wings vibrating like sails in a hurricane, blue light exploding from between Mab's sharp teeth. A pair of green eyes grew wide. Mab swallowed and gasped. A moment more the witch remained suspended, a languid wind chime, bereft of air. But Fairy was gone and her magic as well. A circling raven, black blot upon the perfect sky, laughed to see Mab resume her graceless fall.

as there another miracle; a wondrous rescue? No. Mab crashed. More than a thud; somewhat less than a thump. All breath exploded from her lungs. Fairy was vomited forth. Disgust etched her blue face as she fled aloft. Mab's mind visited a realm of spiraling corridors, quavering sirens and ill-tended machinery. Slowly, she became aware of lying in a watery hole that fitted her as well as a bespoken grave.

Sparkling clouds of bright-winged insects speckled the humid air, humming at her clogged ears. Foul water perfumed her mouth; agony waltzed through her limbs. She strained to sit up in a soup of algae and duckweed; staring curiously at her body, pleased to discover it remaining in one piece. Satisfied that nothing was missing, she collapsed for an hour, resting and wishing the pain to wash away.

Eventually, the ever resilient witch began to free herself, pulling, pushing with hands and feet; raising malign, bubbling odors with every sucking move through the muck of a great bog. She imagined herself navigating the digestive tract of a nightmare behemoth. Finally, a stretch of open water cradled her, a respite soon interrupted by a familiar and unwelcome voice.

There once was a fox in the lake,
tying knots in the ancient snake,
and on the water
walked the snake's daughter,
while the fox took his usual take.

Mab lifted a head adorned with lily pads. Fox greeted her, drifting lazily in a white birch bark canoe. Mab floated face up, eyes filled with sky. A golden butterfly alighted on her streaming hair. Her ears hid underwater, muffling both Fox's words and the incessant chatter of solicitous insects.

"Well done. You are probably the first person to survive a fall from the moon. Know where you are? Don't quite feel like talking yet? Here— pick a card. Never mind. Let me."

Fox pulled the Dragon card from his deck, then followed with the Fairy.

"Just as predicted. Fire conjoined with Air and crossed with the flight of the Witch. And now— " Fox closed his eyes and drew the Turtle. "Dismal Swamp, home of Old Snapper, in whose domain we now trespass. None have ever escaped this place. Unless you have wings. Or a canoe crafted of sacred white birch. Like this one. Sorry, can't take you aboard— it's that old white magic, black magic conundrum— oil and water, they just don't mix.

"Legend holds that the only way out of Dismal Swamp is through Old Snapper's gullet. However, I suspect that a resourceful enchantress might strike a better bargain. You need only dive down here to find him. The old boy is quite the recluse. Oh no— no quitting now. You're in far too deep for that," Fox cheerily concluded and began to paddle away. But a cold regard in Mab's green eyes compelled him to pause.

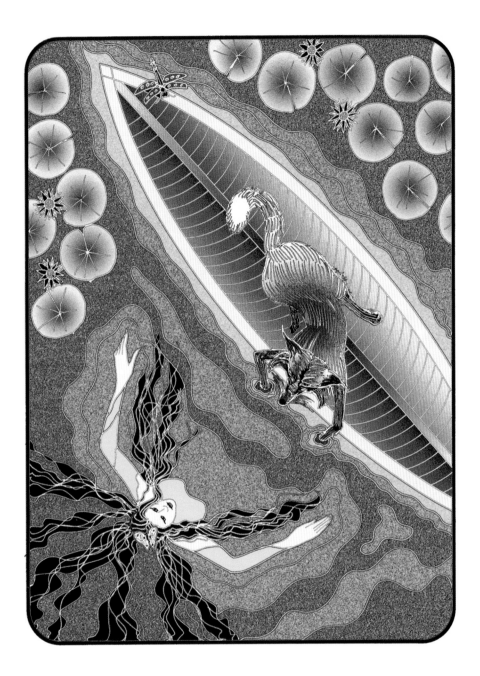

"She wants to know what it all means?" Fox put the question for her, then another. "Dragon spoke of me?"

"He would renew an acquaintance," Mab murmured, lips cresting the surface.

She could not see the card that fell from Fox's deck to the ribbed spine of the canoe. Skull-faced Death. Fox threw a worried glance Mab's way and slapped paddle to water, splashing away.

*t*here was nothing else to do. Far below, someone waited for her. Mab turned over and disappeared under the water without a sound. As she descended the water grew dark and chill. A sagacious carp swam by.

"Tell me about Old Snapper," Mab pleaded and this is what he said to her:

> *Old Snapper's sacred carapace,*
> *bejeweled and baptized, embraced*
> *in water of the eternal rivers,*
> *bathing his carved stigmata,*
> *depicting the way of the world.*

Mab complimented him for his fine words and then sought the advice of what she hoped would prove a more practical minded catfish. This is what that whiskered scavenger revealed:

"Old Snapper is the eldest of dwellers in the water. A sunken vault of primal knowledge. He will answer a single question from the humble supplicant. Thereupon he will catalog the taste of you in the front of his memory. Us he devours. He will..."

As the speech showed no sign of conclusion, Mab wearily resumed her journey toward the bottom of the moss-green swamp, still resolved to locate Old Snapper. Instead, he found her. His piggish snout, swift as a pickpocket and ambitious to sample her legs, thrust forth on a thick, pleated neck. Mab swept herself away. He did not pursue, but waited patiently on the swamp bed, knowing she must come to him.

She held out her left hand; an unnecessary display of her credentials, signaling a pause in their negotiations while she pondered what her question should be. Was it infinite sadness that she sensed in him? Or was it mere hunger for his first witch spiced with envy of Dragon's ancient monopoly? No matter. There was only one possible question and Mab asked it. The great turtle opened his mouth in the manner of one used to having his food willingly surrender to his need. A long, snaketail tongue issued forth. She spied the answer on the tip of his tongue. How to get it? Greedy eyes beckoned her. Mab swam straight to him, somersaulting and settling upon his ridge-backed shell. He stretched his neck backward to get at her. Mab leaned back, avoiding the deadly beak. His gaping mouth taught her how to work the theft. Mab placed a tantalizing hand near each of his pivoting eyes. The trick: bait him with both hands; thieve the truth with one before he snapped at the other. Was he utterly beguiled by the delicately waving fingers? Was he aware of her left hand within his trapdoor maw? She had her answer and should have been safely away. No! She would not play Mab the Cheat. Her hand lingered a moment too long as she knew it must. In that terrible instant, the razor jaws closed. Mab got her hand free but at the cost of her snake-born eleventh finger.

Darkness slammed like a coffin lid upon her head. Reeking water stopped her mouth

and ears. A horrible, hissing voice ordered Mab conscripted in the legions of the drowned. Claws yanked her hair, pulling her away. She arose from the depths, belly up, dead white fish flesh, black hair spread like a death bed comforter, and, instead of copper pennies to quiet her eyes, a pair of conspiratorial leeches explored her pale cheek and brow. And far below, an old turtle shuddered.

o hideous claw but a plain and sturdy maternal hand it was that had dragged Mab from Dismal Swamp. She awoke on a bed of dried marigolds. Her left hand had finished bleeding upon parched ground, her resting place bannered by a broad purple stain. Mab's wincing eyes perceived a veiled lady, short and stout, kneeling above her, shadowed under a baleful sky framing a blood-clotted sun. A sickle gleamed in stubby fingers. The other hand grasped a skein of Mab's hair.

"We must do something about this wild hair of yours, child. It is a haven for mushrooms and snails and spiders. You stink of fish. A thorough washing and severe cut are in order."

Strong hands hoisted Mab as if she were no more than a newborn.

"My hair cannot be cut," Mab wailed, face knotted in a sudden fit of hysteria. She could not explain the ancient paradox that the hair of a witch can only be sheared by a fatal blade of pure silver, but that silver cannot hold an edge sufficiently sharp to perform the act. She fumbled with her mangled hand to pull a rope of hair through her mouth, clamping down with her teeth. The Veiled Lady cupped Mab's face in her hands, catching a squall of salt tears.

"Do not bite your hair. It is unseemly."

"My hand! My hand!"

"This will make you feel better," soothed the Veiled Lady, wrapping the awful wound in a poultice of alder leaves and cobwebs.

"What business did you have with Dragon, Fairy and Old Snapper? It must have been very important to give up your life," the Veiled Lady inquired as she applied to Mab's hair a brush with bristles of wire. Mab sobbed the story that began with Fox's game on the Eve of Allhallows.

"But you see I did not give up my life."

The Veiled Lady traced a semblance of the witch's face upon the blood-stained ground. As Mab watched, fault lines propagated across the sketch like wrinkles upon the face of a crone. The crone withered to a skull. Then a hellish breeze blew the picture to dust.

"The sign of Death. Most conclusive," the Veiled Lady made her pronouncement.

"What must I do? Help me," Mab pleaded, eyes flooding once more with bitter tears.

"I am helping you, darling Maybelle. I am preparing you to enter the realm of Death," the lady said, touching her fingertips in final benediction upon Mab's whitened forehead.

"Now for your hair. My old sickle of common pig iron will do. How am I to reach the top of your head? You are so much taller than I. But, no, first you must be cleansed."

Mab was subjected to a soaking spray and scrub with crabapple vinegar. Then she was clothed in a soft robe. The Veiled Lady concluded that the cutting could only be accomplished by climbing upon Mab's back. Therefore, Mab groaned and shook at what seemed to be the weight of the world. With each stroke of the

sickle, Mab began sinking into the ground. By the time the Veiled Lady was knee deep in a pile of orphaned, raven tresses, Mab had disappeared from mortal sight.

"Well that is most odd," mused the Veiled Lady. "I have never seen the like."

This she said because her final glimpse of the witch showed that the length of her hair had not changed.

ab drifted down through the layered ages of the world. She arrived in a long corridor. Lacking other purpose, she began walking. Someone tall, bearing a riot of dark hair and painfully thin from many missed meals, approached from the far end. The stranger's hair and robe were the image of her own, but from under the crown of black hair stared a skull. Mab's hands crossed her breast in surprise. The skeleton apologetically crossed a pair of brittle hands over the hole in a chest where once a heart had lodged. Mab touched her own face, relieved to discover familiar skin. The skeleton grimly mimicked her, bony hand to hollow cheek.

"Who are you?" Mab asked.

The skeleton's mouth gaped. Words tumbled out like gold coins pricked from a miser's purse.

"The Dragon old," mumbled Dragon in his restive sleep.

"The Fairy cold." The skeleton played ventriloquist dummy to Fairy's music.

"Count each ancient emblem." Fox's tongue flickered between empty jaws.

"The Turtle jailed." Three purloined words drifting across distant waters.

"The Lady veiled." A puzzled voice, still pondering the matter of Mab's hair.

The skeleton gestured to Mab.

"A witch's hand to bind them," she answered.

Now the skeleton spoke in muted tones, which Mab knew was the voice of Death itself.

"Touched by fire, fallen through air, drowned in water, laid to rest in earth. Soul snatcher Mab, dead before your allotted time. How many souls have you cheated me? Now, I take yours."

Mab caught a fugitive trace of luminescence in the depths of the skull's eye sockets. Searching deeply therein, she was startled by a scene of lambent pageantry— a procession illuminated by fugitive fireflies from a summer night. She witnessed a dancing witch chased by a swift fox, the fox tracked by a swooping raven, the raven stalked by a limping wizard. Then the witch hunted the wizard to complete a merry circle of laughing fools. The vision dissolved at a loud moan from Mab's stomach, making her cry out. Death shook the colors from its hollow head, trying to restore a pious gloom.

"If I am dead, then why am I starving? Would you happen to have a fat, luscious tomato? A crust of bread? A small green olive?"

Death hastily reached out to her, a bleached hand summoning Mab to forlorn betrothal.

"Are you forgetting? A witch's hand to bind them," Mab smiled and shook her head. "I may not know what that means but— look!"

She pointed to the banded snake crawling out of the skeleton's sleeve and up the wrist. Could a dead fossil face betray such surprise?

"Well hello little friend. It seems such a long time since I left you in Old Snapper's belly."

Mab touched the fingers of bone. The snake crossed over to Mab, coiling around her

wrist. Snake and witch explored each other's eyes as they had done long ago. An old understanding was shared, and the snake, once more, became the finger. Life blood pulsed in her veins again.

"It seems that I am not quite dead. Shall we say good-bye for now?" Mab demanded, but she spoke to no one, instead, standing solitary in a night forest shrouded by a cold mist.

ᵐab's bare feet told her that she stood in a copse of crooked, leafless trees not far from her house. As she lingered uncertainly, Raven latched onto her shoulder with unclean talons.

"PIECES OF EIGHT! PIECES OF EIGHT! My parrot impression. I've been practicing. What do you think?"

Mab's left hand curled like a snake, ready to seize the bird's throat. She resisted temptation, knowing she should hear Raven's words.

"Know what it means? No? Let me tell you. PIECES OF WHAT I JUST ATE!" Raven laughed and hopped on top of her head.

"Such delicious looking eyes. Which shall it be— right or left? A plague of sudden wealth. Tasty indecision. Which shall it be?"

"Wouldn't you prefer to be raking over some ripe carcass?"

"A common misconception, Mistress Witch. My tastes are eclectic. Rancid carrion or living delicacy— no difference," the raven coughed in her face. "Pardon me. Persistent rasp. All these cold, damp mornings and diet of uncured meat. To return to the matter at hand. My master"— Raven coughed and spat the word— "requires that I enforce your attendance upon his pleasure. Naturally, there is a fee for my trouble. One of your delectable, green eyes."

Mab appeared to give the demand serious thought, as if value were hidden deeply therein.

"Who is your master?"

"That answer will cost your other eye. But do not make me the cause of your stumbling in darkness for the remainder of a miserable life. My guilt would be unbearable," Raven replied, his razor beak hovering over her brow.

"Very well. It seems I have no choice," Mab conceded. "But I must know— have we met? Or is there one who shares your countenance?"

Raven's feathers ruffled in anger.

"You know the answer full well, Witch. Long ago, you took the life of my brother."

"Oh yes," Mab smiled. "A pair of ravens disturbed a witch at her twilight prayers with their vulgar noise. What happened then? Recite to me what your sharp eyes captured."

"Witch stoops for stone. Closes one eye. Left hand throws stone. Brother's skull split. Soul snatched. I fly, dishonoring his death by not picking his bones clean."

"At times," Mab reflected, "I regret not having closed both eyes and gotten you as well. So be it. You mentioned your fee? Take it. One of my eyes. As you know, I need but one."

Mab folded her arms and tilted her head upward. Raven croaked triumphantly and prepared to strike. He hesitated.

"I must beg a point of clarification Mistress. Do you mean to kill me?

"Oh, that answer has a price," Mab replied. "I would know your master's whereabouts. And I have questions concerning a fox with whom I suspect you have close acquaintance."

But a crimson shadow passed by.
Stifled squawk. Eruption of feathers.
Fox had Raven in his mouth. He gave
the bird a neck-snapping shake, dropped
the body and savagely exulted:

There once was a fox and a raven,
One sly and the other craven,
Enemies of old,
The bird dead and cold,
The fox just misbehavin'.

ox fled with his prize. Mab followed, scent of fox tail and Raven's cold blood leading her homeward. The sky was slashed by a foggy sliver of moon and pockmarked with northern clouds, promising a cold, wet dawn. Soon, the silhouette of her house rose up like a spinster's hump on the bankside above the bridge. She approached the place where she had first met Fox, and found a small, iron-barred cage housing him. He peered out with anxious eyes. Next to the cage lay the hat wherein Mab's journey had begun. Raven drooped nearby, a broken shadow. A circle had been scratched upon the damp ground. A line of cards, faces down, decorated the perimeter. Mab knelt, turning and flipping each one, revealing Fox, Dragon, Fairy, Turtle, Veiled Lady, Death, Raven and Wizard. The Queen of Clubs fell from her sleeve. She arranged it with the others.

> *The Dragon old, the Fairy cold,*
> *Count each ancient emblem.*
> *The Turtle jailed, the Lady veiled,*
> *A witch's hand to bind them.*

Fox had not spoken. Rather it was the figure who limped from the shadows of the bridge. Mab recognized the gray-bearded wizard whom she had seen in Death's eyes. A spired crown bound his head. A gnarled, oaken staff was gripped in thin fists. This he touched to the circle and sudden, blue flames ringed Mab.

"A witch is born, a wizard made," Wizard intoned, eyes bleary behind thick spectacles.

"Silence! Nothing vexes me as much as a woman's voice," he shook an imperious finger at her. "Shall I educate you, Mistress Witch?"

Mab scoured her brain in search of a rhyme for pompous. Nonplused, she idly allowed the blue flames to play about her left hand. Fox would know. He was good at that sort of thing.

"You know well the avatars of fire, air, water and earth, but what of him who revealed their secret, the secret of the ancient verse? There lies, in a southern desert, a fallen marble column whereon those words are engraved, their meaning swept by the sands of the ages. Who dare explore the buried tomb on which that column had toppled? Who but myself? There I uncovered a shattered granite tablet inscribed with runes of a lost epoch. A daunting maze of fragments, yet I restored the lost knowledge. Envision the origin of the world. Four elementals contending for dominion. None could prevail. All was chaos. A witch came to them. She spoke enchanting words, causing them to dwell as living beings upon the world and end their eternal strife. So. What do we have? Ancestral myth? Prophecy? Both? One secret remains. Yours. Now speak."

Mab yawned. And stuck out her tongue.

"To be expected," Wizard shook his head. "She masters the elements, drinking deeply the universal mystery, yet learns nothing, knows not what she has done. So be it. A touch of my staff relieves you of your unearned gift— that primal magic enhancing your pitiful witchcraft."

Wizard raised the staff with both arms above his head in solemn ritual.

"I must cleanse his muddled vision," Mab decided. She stepped through the ring of blue flame. A sprig of evergreen rue appeared in her fingers. Her clever hands stole his glasses, softly clasping his face and rubbing the leaves upon his eyes. Mab sang an old puzzlement:

"GUESS WHO!?"

izard struggled for a moment, then relaxed as if soothed by a mother's touch. Mab spun him about. He staggered, tripped over his oaken staff, fell into the hat on the ground and vanished.

"Oh my!" said Mab. "It seems Dragon will have to make do with a wizard in place of a fox."

A smile tweaking the corners of her mouth, a quiet laugh tickling her heart, Mab picked up the hat and sent it sailing downstream, watching until it disappeared around a grassy bend. She turned to go home, noticing the door of the cage hanging open. Fox had escaped yet again. Morning drifted down on silver sheets of chilling mist. Mab's toe snagged on a dead thing. The empty sack. She picked it up, wrung out a stale stream of water and strolled home. A commotion at her kitchen window forced her eyes up in time to spy Fox losing his grip on a creaky shutter. The moment stretched exquisitely. Mab leisurely shook out the sack and opened it to receive him as tenderly as love on a spring morning. She savored the horror in his eyes, the muffled cry of despair, the odor of animal panic trapped in a sack. Mab peered inside, raindrops coursing down her nose. His thin black arms clutched three eggs and a bottle of hand-pressed May wine.

"Mab! I was just looking for you."

"You may address me as 'Sorceress whose dwelling I have entered without bidding because I deem my life worthless.'"

"Yes, oh Sorceress, I can explain. But first— would you care for a snack? Have you ever tasted an omelet sauteed in red wine? This recipe happens to call for stolen eggs, so— "

"I have been kidnapped, dropped on moon and earth. Finger bitten off. Drowned. Nearly blinded. Even bored. Am I forgetting anything?"

"Some day you and I shall look back and laugh at this whole affair," Fox sighed. "I confess all. An unfortunate business with that villain. He was nothing more than a cheap magician— rabbit-in-hat, saw-you-in-half sort of thing."

"He possessed trappings of wizardry."

"True," Fox allowed. "Yes, trappings. Would it surprise you to learn that I once committed a borrowing from Dragon? In the spirit of scientific inquiry. Do you know that a dragon's touch imparts the most unexpected thaumaturgic properties? That hat— direct portal to his den. Amazing, yes? A treasury overflowing with potent, mystical paraphernalia. Well, I happened to fall in with this would-be conjuror. Supplying him the odd trinket. But never enough. Who knew his avarice would beget darker ambitions? So there I was— caught between peevish Dragon and crazed Wizard, each threatening me agonizing death. I needed an ally. What to do?"

"Trick a witch and die a third time?"

"Ha! Funny. Still a sense of humor. I view our involvement as a delightful whim of fate. You help me. I help you. Every step into hazard, there I was, at your side. Legends will sing of

Mab, Mistress of Death itself. And maybe a verse reserved for her partner, the clever Fox. Shall we celebrate?"

Mab weighed the quaint balance of life; her falling into Fox's hat and now he into her sack. A tangle of thorn-sharp longings glinted in her green eyes.

"Yes. Let's," she closed the sack on his face, swung it over her back, brushed back her sodden hair and went inside.

The King is dead,

The Queen abed,

Each of these a Blessing.

The Maid dismayed,

The Knave well flayed,

Time to leave off jesting.

The Dragon old,

The Fairy cold,

Count each ancient Emblem.

The Turtle jailed,

The Lady veiled,

A Witch's hand to bind them.